www.enchantedlionbooks.com

First Reprint Edition published in 2017 by Enchanted Lion Books,
67 West Street, 317A, Brooklyn, New York 11222
Copyright © 1959 by Jacqueline Ayer
Rights arranged with the estate of Jacqueline Ayer
Color restoration and layout: Marc Drumwright
Originally published in 1959 by Harcourt, Brace and Company, New York, New York
All rights reserved under International and Pan-American Copyright Conventions
A CIP record is on file with the Library of Congress
Printed in China in February 2017 by RR Donnelley Asia Printing Solutions Limited
ISBN: 978-1-59270-231-2
1 3 5 7 9 8 6 4 2

Nu Dang and His Kite

Jacqueline Ayer

Nu Dang and His Kite

Enchanted Lion Books, New York

IN a sunny, sleepy place
halfway around the world in Siam,
on the banks of a long brown river,
there once lived a little boy
whose name was Nu Dang.

He loved more than anything else—
more than swimming in the cool river on a hot day,
more than orange ice,
even more than two orange ices—
most and best Nu Dang loved to fly his kite.

Whenever the day was right for kites—
when the wind was strong,
the sky clear,
and the sun shining brightly—
Nu Dang and his friends
would come with their kites to a grassy field.

Nu Dang's kite was the boldest and the bravest of them all.
It ran swiftly with the wind
and chased the birds that flew around the sun.
Nu Dang was the happiest boy in the grassy field.
He was the happiest boy in Siam.
He was the happiest boy in the world.
Nu Dang was just that happy.

And what beautiful and brave kites they were!
Kites that were birds,
kites that were snakes,
kites that were fish,
kites that were demons and gods.
The wind pulled them all high up into the sky.

One day, after many days of wind and kites
and clear blue skies,
Nu Dang lost his kite!
Just like that—slip!—
the string left his hand
and his kite disappeared.
Nu Dang went to the river,
climbed into his small boat,
and sat, drifting sadly
and thinking about his kite.
What a bold and bad kite it was
to have left him and run off with the wind!
He was a little angry.
But what a brave and beautiful kite it was!
He was very sad.
He looked in all the corners of the sky.
No kite at all.
Nowhere. Not anywhere. No kite at all.
He must find it.
So Nu Dang picked up his paddle
and set off down the long brown river
to find his kite.

Out on the big river, he came first
to a vendor of sweet cakes and colored water.
"Have you seen my kite?"
But the vendor was much too busy
to notice a lost kite.
Nowhere. Not anywhere. No kite at all.

Nu Dang asked a boatman,
with a heap of fresh hay for his oxen,
and he hadn't seen the kite.
Nowhere. Not anywhere. No kite at all.

Nu Dang asked the boatbusman and his ticket taker,
and they hadn't seen his kite.
Nowhere. Not anywhere. No kite at all.

Nu Dang passed a group of young priests,
and politely, with a proper bow,
he interrupted their studies.
But they hadn't seen his kite.
Nowhere. Not anywhere. No kite at all.

Nu Dang came to a great, noisy crowd of boats.
It was the "Floating Market."
He paddled carefully and asked his question quietly.
Everyone was brisk and busy
and had no time for a small boy
with questions about a kite.

Still, he asked everyone:
the vendor of lotus and jasmine,
and the vendor of curry sauce and chilies.
He asked the pineapple, pomelo, and papaya boat;
the chickpea-green bean boat;
the "all kinds of fresh fish" boat.
And they all said, "No!"
They hadn't seen his kite.

Nu Dang asked the merchant
who sold green and yellow mangoes.
He asked the spice vendor and the flower vendor.
He asked the pork butcher.
He even asked the pork butcher's dog,
who was sunning himself and dozing.
He asked everyone.
And they all said, "No!"
Nowhere. Not anywhere. No kite at all.

Nu Dang was beginning to feel like crying,
and he paddled slowly and sadly,
looking for his kite up in the clouds.

Oof! He bumped into a huge rice barge.
His friend Pranee laughed down at him.
"*Arai*, Nu Dang?
What's wrong, little red mouse?"
"Oh, Pranee, I've lost my beautiful kite."
"*Mai pen rai*," she said.

"No matter, you can get another."
"Not ever another. Not ever another
as bold and brave!" answered Nu Dang.
And before his tears came, he rushed off
past the line of rice barges making
their slow and heavy way to the city.

Nu Dang turned off the big river
into a small and winding canal.
At the restaurant boat, which was
steaming with good smells
and gleaming with shiny brass pots,
he asked for his kite.
But nobody had seen it.
Nowhere. Not anywhere. No kite at all.

Nu Dang came to an old farmhouse.
There seemed to be no one at home—
except for the ducks,
the chickens,
a litter of new puppies,
a family of cats,
and a large, very grand rooster.
The rooster shook his head, as much as
to say none of them had seen anything.
Nowhere. Not anywhere. No kite at all.

แหลมทองบริษัทจำกัด

พายเรือเร็ว

福洋東

Farther along, the banks of the
small stream were crowded with
shops and signs, banners and lanterns,
all perched high over the river on stilts.
Nu Dang asked at the tailor's shop,
at the Indian cloth merchant's,
and at the Chinese cookshop.
And no one, not anyone, had seen his kite.
Nowhere. Not anywhere. No kite at all.

Here at last was his own house.
In the early evening quiet not a leaf moved,
not a petal of the tiniest flower stirred.
There was almost no wind at all.
And then above his head, he heard a quiet
flap, flap, flap.

And there it was!
Nu Dang's kite was
falling and bobbing, wilted and tired,
down to the ground.
It had run and run and run with the wind.
But as the wind grew gentler,
it flipped and flopped and floated down.
And then the kind wind caught it once more
and carried it slowly home.

Nu Dang was the happiest boy
who ever had a kite.
He was the happiest boy in Siam.
He was the happiest boy in the world.
Nu Dang was just that happy.